6/02

SANTA MARIA PUBLIC LIBRARY

3 2113 00448 0615

D0578997

For my friend Nikki Grimes
who pointed me in the right direction

Copyright © 2001 by Julie Mammano.
All rights reserved.

Book design by Lucy Nielsen.
Typeset in Gill Sans and ITC Officina.
The illustrations in this book were rendered in watercolor.
Printed in Hong Kong.

Library of Congress Cataloging-in-Publication Data
Mammano, Julie.
Rhinos who play soccer / by Julie Mammano.
p. cm.
Summary: Rhinoceroses play a game of soccer as Team Rhino meets the
All Stars. Includes a list of soccer vocabulary.
ISBN 0-8118-2779-8
[1. Soccer—Fiction. 2. Rhinoceroses—Fiction.] I. Title.
PZ7.M3115 Rc 2001
[E]--dc21
00-011180

Distributed in Canada by Raincoast Books
9050 Shaughnessy Street, Vancouver, British Columbia V6P 6E5

10 9 8 7 6 5 4 3 2 1

Chronicle Books LLC
85 Second Street, San Francisco, California 94105

www.chroniclebooks.com/Kids

Rhinos Who Play Soccer

JULIE MAMMANO

chronicle books · san francisco

They HOOK UP with a CREW called the All Stars

for a friendly game of FOOTIE.

BAM!

They **DRIBBLE** with fancy footwork. They **CHURN THE TURF.**

They LOFT PRIMO **AIR-SHREDDING** kicks.

HEADS UP!

They
jump
and
bump.

They
MARK UP
head to head
and toe to toe.

Team
Rhino
blasts

a RAD
MONSTER
STRIKE.

Rhinos who play soccer go for a **DIVING HEADER.**

THUD!

They **TAKE IT ON THE GRILL** and **EAT IT BIG TIME.**

Sometimes the action gets totally GNARLY when the All Stars

The All Stars make a FAKE HEEL-BACK CROSS PASS to sneak a sly

They **HAMMER** the ball toward the goal.

What a SAVE!

The KEEPER owns the net and blocks the shot.

The All Stars **RULE.** Rhinos who play soccer are good sports.

After they GIVE PROPS to the victors, it's time for a . . .

REMATCH!

Turf Talk

hook up to meet

crew a group

footie nickname for soccer; also called football and futbol

kick off the kick that starts the game or restarts it after halftime and goals

pitch playing field

dribble to run while kicking the ball

churn the turf to run or dribble at high speed

heads up watch out

loft to make the ball go really high

primo the best

air shredding gravity-defying kicks and moves

mark up to guard a person on the other team

defense the team trying to get the ball back, while keeping the other team from scoring

pass to kick the ball to your teammate

breakaway to dribble toward the goal while the other team isn't in the way

rad really good

monster strike a powerful kick toward the goal

sink it deep to score a goal deep in the net

goal to score a point

hotshot a really good player

pounded to fall down really hard

diving header to hit the ball with your head while diving for it

take it on the grill to fall on your face

eat it to fall or crash

big time really

gnarly bad, scary

tackle to take away the ball from the other team

fake a pretend kick or pass

heel-back cross pass a backwards kick across the field

hammer to kick the ball really hard

save to keep the ball from going into the net

keeper the person who keeps the ball out of the net

attack to try for a goal

boot it to kick

got game to play really well

toast to lose the game

rule to win, be the best

give props to say "hooray" to the winning team

rematch to play another game